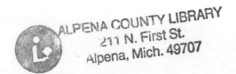

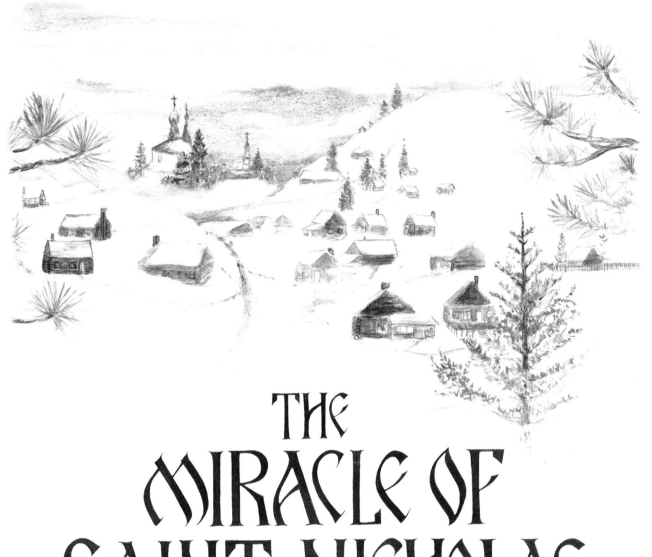

THE MIRACLE OF SAINT NICHOLAS

by Gloria Whelan

illustrated by Judith Brown

BETHLEHEM BOOKS · IGNATIUS PRESS
WARSAW, N.D.   SAN FRANC

The illustrations for this book were done in egg tempera, a technique traditionally used in the painting (or writing) of icons. The display type (cover and title page) and drop caps were hand lettered by the illustrator using the same technique. The text is set in Adobe® Minion Multiple Master and Minion Multiple Master Expert.

Color illustrations © 1997 by Judith Brown
Text © 1997 by Gloria Whelan

ISBN 1-883937-18-3
Library of Congress catalog number: 97-73496

Cover art by Judith Brown
Book and cover design by Lydia Reynolds

Bethlehem Books • Ignatius Press
15605 County Road 15, Minto, ND 58261

Printed in Canada ∞

In memory of Joan Couzens

IT WAS THE DAY before Christmas in the small Russian village of Zeema. Alexi's babushka was telling Alexi what Christmas was like when she was a girl. "Our church was as crowded as a pod full of peas. Pine boughs filled the church with the scent of the forest. Candles made the church as bright as the sunniest day. Watching over us was the blessed icon of St. Nicholas."

"What is an icon?" Alexi asked. A question always sat on the tip of Alexi's tongue like a little bird ready to fly.

"An icon is a painting of a holy person. It is a painting into which the artist has put his whole soul. Our icon of St. Nicholas was five hundred years old. It was more precious to us than our lives."

"BABUSHKA," Alexi asked, "Why is our church closed?"

"When I was a child, the very age you are now," the Babushka said, "soldiers came to our village. They did not like churches. They did not want people to believe in God. They warned the villagers, 'If we find you in your church we will arrest you and send you far away.' No sooner had the soldiers barred the doors of St. Nicholas than everything inside the church disappeared. It is a great mystery."

7

"THAT WAS LONG AGO," the Babushka said. "Now the soldiers who closed our church are gone."

Alexi asked, "Then why can't we celebrate Christmas tomorrow in St. Nicholas?"

"The church has been empty for sixty years," the Babushka said. "You cannot celebrate Christmas in a church with an empty altar, with no cross, no candles, no bread or wine, no icon of St. Nicholas and no priest. Birds have made their nests there. It is dancing with mice. It would take a miracle to open our church."

"Babushka, what is a miracle?" Alexi asked.

"A miracle happens," his babushka said, "When God enters into your dream. But first you must have the dream."

THAT AFTERNOON Alexi rubbed the frost from the windows of St. Nicholas and peered inside. The church was empty. The floor was soft with dust. The walls were netted with cobwebs. He tried the door of the church. It was unlocked. If a door were unlocked, Alexi was a boy to walk through it.

The startled mice scampered out of the church. As Alexi stood inside the deserted church he said to himself, "I wish we could celebrate Christmas here." When Alexi set his heart on something he moved as quickly as the mice.

He wrapped a bundle of twigs with some twine and swept dust from the floor. He brushed the cobwebs from the walls. He cleaned away the birds' nests.

Alexi tramped through the snow to the pine forest at the edge of the village. The wind tried to snatch away his cap. The snow sneaked into the holes in his boots. Reaching up into the trees Alexi broke off some fragrant branches. Returning to the church he laid the boughs around the altar.

ZEEMA WAS A VILLAGE where you were as likely to be in your neighbor's house as your own. Word of what Alexi was doing soon spread through the village.

The villagers hurried to see for themselves. The farmer, the carpenter, the storekeeper, the teacher, and the shoemaker arrived with their families. Alexi's mother and father came with Alexi's babushka and his little sister, Natasha. Natasha brought her stuffed bear who would not be left behind.

One after another the whole village took turns peeking into the church. One after another they returned to their homes with a big smile and a little secret.

ONLY THE SHOEMAKER stayed behind. He was a quiet old man with gentle ways. His clothes were worn and patched. His gray beard was tangled. His shoulders were stooped from hunching over his work. His hands were stained from tanning leather.

The shoemaker asked Alexi, "Why have you swept out the church and laid the pine boughs about?"

"So we can celebrate Christmas in the church tomorrow," Alexi answered.

"Many times I have mended your boots, Alexi. When I saw all the holes you had worn in them, I said to myself, 'There is a boy who will always be one step ahead of us.'"

The shoemaker went away with a little smile and a big secret.

FOR THEIR DINNER on Christmas Eve Alexi's family had jam to put into their tea. There was a dish of cooked, dried fruits, twelve fruits in all, one for each of the apostles. Alexi's mother had prepared kutya, a thick porridge made of crushed hazelnuts and almonds cooked with barley and honey. It had bubbled to itself on the stove all afternoon. "You can tell when it is done," Alexi's mother said, "When it does not talk anymore."

Alexi's father scattered straw on the floor to remind them that Jesus was born in a stable. He put a bit of hay under the tablecloth to remind them Jesus lay in a manger.

Outside the wind sent the snow tumbling and swirling. It sought out the cracks in Alexi's house. It sent bits of surprised snow through the cracks. Still Alexi and his family were happy, for the porridge warmed their insides and the stove warmed their outsides.

FTER DINNER there were gifts. Alexi received new boots. They would protect his feet from the snow that had nothing better to do than fall day after day. Natasha was given a sweater to shield her from the cold winds that rushed down from the North Pole. As she did every Christmas Eve, the Babushka gave Alexi and Natasha a gingerbread man baked with her precious store of molasses.

It was time to go to bed. Alexi's mother told him, "You must lie down like a stone and rise up like new bread."

In bed that night Alexi could not stop thinking of the empty church. He watched the moon turn the snow blue and the icicles golden. He climbed out from under his warm quilt.

ALEXI PUT ON HIS NEW BOOTS and went out into the winter night. He tramped through the snow until he reached the church of St. Nicholas. If a miracle was going to happen, Alexi wanted to be there.

He was surprised to find the farmer and his family inside the church. The farmer was placing two silver candlesticks upon the altar. His wife had a handful of candles. As the flames kindled on the altar, the dark hurried away.

"Where did the candles and candlesticks come from?" Alexi asked.

The farmer explained, "The day the church was closed my father concealed the candlesticks in a sack of grain."

"Every summer when we gathered the honey," his wife said, "I made candles from the bees' wax for just such a day as this one."

THE TEACHER entered the church. She opened a lumpy bundle. Inside the bundle was a cloth woven with many hues, as though bright birds had flown back and forth leaving behind their colors. The teacher spread the cloth over the altar.

"Where did so beautiful a cloth come from?" Alexi asked.

The teacher said, "When the church was closed my mother hid the cloth among our quilts."

There was the carpenter and his family. The carpenter was holding a cross. "My dedushka rescued this cross from the church the day St. Nicholas was closed," the carpenter said. "All these years it has lain hidden under the floor of my workshop."

The storekeeper and his wife arrived carrying a bottle of wine and a basket of bread. "For many years I have saved this wine," the storekeeper told Alexi.

The wife of the storekeeper said, "I have baked loaves of the holy Christmas bread and marked them with the sign of the cross."

J UST THEN Alexi's mother and father along with his babushka and Natasha entered the church. Natasha was yawning for it was very early in the morning. The Babushka looked stern and happy all at once. She was carrying something wrapped up in her best shawl. The villagers crowded around her.

Gently she unfolded the scarf. There was the painting of St. Nicholas. At last the icon was in the church where it had been for as many years as anyone could recall. The eyes of the saint seemed to be looking right at Alexi.

ALEXI SAID, "Now we have the candles and the altar cloth, the cross, the bread and wine, and the icon of St. Nicholas, but we don't have a priest."

"We must wait," his babushka said.

Everyone sat quietly in the church. Natasha was asleep with her head on Babushka's shoulder.

The church doors opened. A priest walked down the aisle. He was dressed in a robe of white and gold like sun breaking through morning clouds. In his hands he held the Holy Scriptures.

"It's the shoemaker!" Alexi cried.

BUT HE WAS the shoemaker no longer. His scraggly beard was neatly combed. He did not stoop but stood as straight as a pine tree. His ragged and patched clothes had been changed for the robe of a priest.

The Babushka whispered to Alexi, "Many years ago it was dangerous to be a priest. Priests were often put into prison. So we hid the priest in our village. He became our shoemaker. Now we have our priest back again."

EVERYONE LIT A CANDLE. The church was as bright as a summer day. Watching over the church in a place of honor was the blessed icon of St. Nicholas. And the Christmas service was just as Alexi's babushka remembered.